Xochitl and the Flowers

Xóchitl, la Niña de las Flores

STORY • CUENTO
Jorge Argueta

ILLUSTRATIONS • ILUSTRACIONES
Carl Angel

CHILDREN'S BOOK PRESS / EDITORIAL LIBROS PARA NIÑOS
San Francisco, California

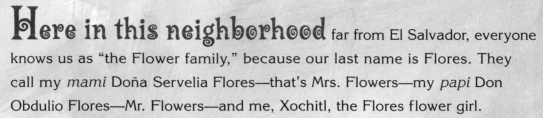

Here in this neighborhood far from El Salvador, everyone knows us as "the Flower family," because our last name is Flores. They call my *mami* Doña Servelia Flores—that's Mrs. Flowers—my *papi* Don Obdulio Flores—Mr. Flowers—and me, Xochitl, the Flores flower girl.

When we lived in El Salvador, my grandfather Rubén cheerfully told me that "Xochitl" means "flower" in the Nahuatl language. "A long, long time ago," he told me, "long before the Spaniards even dreamed of coming to our land, our ancestors—Nahuatl Indians, just like you—lived here. We named you Xochitl in their honor."

En este barrio, lejos de El Salvador, todo el mundo nos conoce como la familia de las flores: A mi mami le dicen doña Servelia Flores, a mi papi le dicen don Obdulio Flores y a mí me dicen Xóchitl, la niña de las flores.

—«Xóchitl» en el idioma náhuatl significa «flor» —me explicaba alegre mi abuelito Rubén cuando vivíamos en El Salvador—. Antes, mucho antes de que los españoles soñaran con llegar a estas tierras, tus antepasados, indios náhuas como tú, ya vivían aquí. Y en honor de ellos te llamas Xóchitl.

In the teeny San Francisco apartment where we live now with our Uncle Benjamin and Aunt Candelaria, I miss El Salvador. I miss the weekends when I sat in our garden with my *mami* and *papi,* arranging bouquets of flowers.

Over there, our flowers made everybody happy. When Fidel married Rosa, we decked out their house like a garden. When Grillito, the shoemaker's dog, died, we made him a big beautiful bouquet. And for Lala Osorio's fifteenth birthday, her family asked us to make fifteen nosegays for her fifteen friends.

En el apartamento chiquitito donde ahora vivimos en San Francisco con el tío Benjamín y la tía Candelaria, me hace falta El Salvador. Extraño los fines de semana cuando me sentaba en el jardín de mi casa con mi papi y mi mami, haciendo ramos de flores.

Allá nuestras flores les daban alegría a todos. Cuando Fidel se casó con Rosa, les adornamos la casa como un jardín. Y cuando murió Grillito, el perro del zapatero, le hicimos un ramo grande y hermoso. También, para la fiesta de quince años de Lala Osorio, su familia nos encargó quince ramos para sus quince damas.

Here, days go by, as slow as turtles. At night, I hear my *mami* tell my *papi* about the flower shop she'd like to have in this country.

My *mami* works every day, cleaning houses with Aunt Candelaria. On weekends, they take me along. My *papi* paints houses or works anywhere he can. And I draw flowers or write letters to grandparents, neighbors, and friends in El Salvador.

In school, I can already say a few sentences in English. I practice them when I'm alone; I probably seem a little crazy when I ask myself, "How are you? My name is Xochitl. Do you like flowers?"

Aquí los días van despacio como las tortugas. De noche, oigo a mi mami que habla con mi papi de la tienda de flores que sueña con tener algún día en este país.

Mi mami trabaja todos los días, limpiando casas con mi tía Candelaria. Los fines de semana me llevan con ellas. Mi papi pinta casas o trabaja de lo que encuentra. Y yo dibujo flores y les escribo cartas a mis abuelitos, vecinos y amiguitos de El Salvador.

En la escuela, ya puedo decir varias oraciones en inglés. Cuando estoy sola las practico y parezco loquita diciendo: —*How are you? My name is Xochitl. Do you like flowers?*

One afternoon, my *mami* brings home a pailful of lovely white roses and red roses, sunflowers, and freckle-faced Stargazer lilies.

"Xochitl, I'm going to sell flowers," she says, and I'm so happy when I see the blossoms that I bounce.

"Can I help you?" I ask.

"Of course, Xochitl," she smiles.

Later that day, my *mami* and I sell flowers on the street. She fills a small bucket with water and sprays of roses. It's light enough for me to carry.

I feel like a butterfly. With the flowers and my *mami* by my side, I have everything I need. In the flowers I see my *abuelitos,* my neighbors, and everything we left behind in El Salvador.

Un día por la tarde mi mami llega con un balde lleno de hermosas rosas blancas y rosas rojas, girasoles y lirios con sus caras pecositas.

—Xóchitl, voy a vender flores —me dice, y al ver las flores salto de alegría.

—¿Te puedo ayudar? —le pregunto.

—Pues claro que sí, Xóchitl —dice y se sonríe.

Esa misma tarde mi mami y yo nos vamos a vender flores por las calles. En un balde pequeño y menos pesado, mi mami pone agua y ramos de rosas para que lo cargue yo.

Me siento como una mariposa. Con las flores y mi mami a mi lado no me falta nada. En las flores veo a mis abuelitos, a mis vecinos y todo lo que dejamos en El Salvador.

We go in and out of restaurants and stores, asking, "Do you want flowers? We have roses, lilies, and sunflowers. Which would you like?"

Every day, we meet more and more neighbors and they get to know us. In the coffee shop on the corner, we make friends with Mr. Awad, the Arab American man with the small eyes and big smile. When Don Prudencio, the *mariachi* guitarist, sees us anywhere at all, he stops to talk. And Doña Ivania, the owner of El Trebol, the restaurant with the glass door, lets us sell flowers to her customers.

I like selling flowers but, when we get home late at night, my *mami* and I have to soak our feet in the tub—that's how tired we are!

Entramos en restaurantes y tiendas, preguntando: —¿Quiere flores? Traemos rosas, lirios, girasoles. ¿De cuáles quiere?

Cada día conocemos más y más vecinos y ellos nos conocen a nosotras. En el cafetín de la esquina, somos amigas de don Awad, el señor árabe americano de ojos pequeños y sonrisa grande. Don Prudencio, el mariachi de la guitarra, cuando nos ve en cualquier sitio, siempre se detiene y se pone a platicar. Y doña Ivania, la dueña del restaurante El Trébol, el que tiene la puerta de vidrio, nos deja entrar a venderles flores a sus clientes.

Me gusta vender flores, pero por la noche, cuando regresamos ya muy tarde a casa, mi mami y yo llenamos la bañera de agua y metemos los pies, ¡porque los tenemos tan cansados!

One Saturday morning, while the three of us arrange flower bouquets, my *papi* tells us, "I've got a big surprise for you."

"Tell me what it is," I beg.

"What is this huge surprise?" my *mami* asks.

My *papi* opens his eyes wide and announces, "I've found an apartment to rent that has a yard in the back. The yard is filled with garbage right now but, if the three of us work hard, we can turn it into a nursery and sell flowers and plants."

"Flowers and plants!" my *mami* and I repeat, both of us at the same time. Afterwards, we're silent; there's so much going through our heads we don't know what to say.

Un sábado por la mañana mientras los tres arreglamos los ramos de flores para venderlos, mi papi nos dice: —Les tengo una gran sorpresa.

—Decime, papito, decime qué es, por favor —le ruego.

—¿Qué sorpresota es ésta? —pregunta mi mami.

Mi papi abre bien grandes los ojos y anuncia: —He encontrado un apartamento que me rentan, que tiene atrás un patio que por ahora está lleno de basura. Pero si los tres trabajamos duro lo podríamos convertir en un vivero para vender plantas y flores.

—¡Plantas y flores! —repetimos juntas mi mami y yo. Después nos quedamos mudas, pensando en mil cosas y sin saber ni qué decir.

No sooner said than done. The next Saturday, my *papi* borrows my Uncle Benjamin's blue truck, and the moving and cleaning begin!

"What a garbage heap!" my *mami* says.

We make three trips to the dump. We throw out tires, pieces of iron, cardboard, glass, sand, part of a bed, and even a refrigerator door . . .

Don Prudencio, who has come to help us out, selects the best pieces of wood. Mr. Awad paints them and makes tables.

Dicho y hecho. El próximo sábado mi tío Benjamín le presta a mi papi su camión azul, y comienza la mudanza y la limpieza.

—¡Qué chiquero! —dice mi mami.

Hacemos tres viajes al basurero. Botamos llantas, pedazos de hierro, cartones, vidrios, arena, pedazos de una cama, una puerta de refrigeradora...

Don Prudencio, que ha venido a ayudar, aparta los pedazos de madera que puedan servir. Don Awad los pinta y los convierte en mesas.

With the big and little stones that a neighbor gives us, we make paths. We bring in soil and arrange little clay frogs. And Doña Ivania gives my *mami* two parakeets as a present, and right away the yard begins to fill with music.

My *mami* is delighted. "It's like magic, this forsaken place coming to life," she says happily. "Now it's clean and pretty, and ready for flowers and plants to come live here!"

Con las piedras grandes y pequeñas que una señora vecina nos regala hacemos caminitos. Ponemos tierra y acomodamos sapitos de barro. Y doña Ivania le regala a mi mami un par de periquitos, que luego comienzan a llenar el lugar de música.

Mi mami está muy contenta. —Como por arte de magia este lugar olvidado vuelve a tomar vida —dice con alegría—. Está limpio y bonito, listo para que vengan a vivir las flores y las plantas.

Early Sunday morning, we buy yellow, white, and red roses. We buy bougainvilleas with blossoms as blue-red as El Salvador evenings, Calla lilies like white trumpets, sunflowers, small green chili plants, and dwarf lemon trees on which ants circle the world in just a few minutes. We buy aloe— magic green stars!—and sweet, oh so sweet, peppermint.

My *papi* paints a sign on a white sheet. It says:

GRAND OPENING DAY SALE!
PRICES YOU CAN'T REFUSE
COME AND GET 'EM!
XOCHITL FLOWERS AND PLANTS

El domingo, tempranito, compramos rosas amarillas, blancas y rojas. Compramos bugambilias de flores moradas como las tardes de El Salvador, lirios Cala que parecen trompetas blancas, girasoles, arbolitos de chiles verdes y limoneros enanos en los que las hormigas les dan la vuelta al mundo en un ratito. Compramos sábilas —mágicas estrellas verdes— y hierbabuena, ¡ay, qué buena!

Mi papi escribe un rótulo en una gran manta blanca. Dice:

GRAN VENTA DE APERTURA HOY
A PRECIOS DE MEJOR ME LO LLEVO
¡VENGA POR LAS SUYAS!
FLORES Y PLANTAS XÓCHITL

Finally everything is ready! Don Prudencio has brought his musician friends. They sing country songs, Mami's favorites.

Balloons of different colors sway in the breeze, among the flowers and plants. A plump and pretty neighbor makes a huge pot of sweet *horchata* drink for the customers who are about to arrive.

Neighbors come in, new friends. Everything is going wonderfully when suddenly, in the midst of all the celebration, a man appears, tall and bearded, his skin the color of ashes.

Por fin, ya todo está listo. Don Prudencio ha traído a sus amigos músicos. Cantan canciones rancheras, las favoritas de mi mami.

Por todos lados, entre las flores y las plantas, se mecen globos de colores. Y una vecina gordita y bonita hace una olla grande de refresco de horchata para los clientes que están por llegar.

Llegan vecinos, nuevos amigos. Todo va de maravilla, cuando de pronto, en medio de la celebración, se aparece un señor alto y barbudo, de piel ceniza.

He has a piece of paper in his hand, and he shouts in an angry voice, "What do you think you're doing here . . . ? What? What? What? This is a residential neighborhood; it's not a place for entertaining strangers!"

He shows us what he's carrying. It's a letter!

"First thing tomorrow morning, I am letting the authorities know what you're up to." He's Don Roberto, the owner of our little lot, and he doesn't want us to set up our business.

"We are honest working people!" my *papi* answers him. But Don Roberto is too angry to listen and he leaves, just like that.

We all have tears in our eyes.

Viene con un papel en la mano y con tono enfurecido dice: —¿Pero qué se han creído ustedes, qué, qué, qué...? Aquí se respeta; ésta es una zona residencial... no es lugar para entretener a toda clase de gente.

Nos muestra lo que lleva en la mano: ¡Es una carta!

—¡Mañana mismo voy a denunciarlos a las autoridades! —Es don Roberto, el dueño del lugar y no quiere que montemos el negocito.

—¡Nosotros somos personas honradas y trabajadoras! —responde mi papi, pero don Roberto está muy enojado. No escucha y simplemente se va.

Todos tenemos lágrimas en los ojos.

23

"This isn't fair!" Don Prudencio says.

"We won't allow this!" my Aunt Candelaria adds.

"We'll fight it," Mr. Awad shouts in the little bit of Spanish he knows.

The neighbors make a circle, putting their heads together as they whisper. Suddenly, one man says, "Doña Candelaria should do the talking."

"Yes, yes!" the neighbors shout. And Doña Ivania adds, "And I'm going home to get something very special."

My *mami,* my *papi,* and I are so sad that we don't even notice when they all leave together.

—¡Esto es una injusticia! —dice don Prudencio.

—¡No lo vamos a permitir! —añade mi tía Candelaria.

—¡Vamos a luchar! —grita don Awad, con su poquito de español.

Los vecinos hacen un círculo y juntando las cabezas hablan en voz baja. De pronto, un señor dice: —¡Que hable doña Candelaria!

—¡Sí, sí! —gritan los vecinos. Y doña Ivania añade: —Pues yo me voy a mi casa a buscar algo muy especial...

Mi mami, mi papi y yo estamos tan tristes que ni nos fijamos cuando se marchan todos juntos.

Hours later, while my *mami*, my *papi*, and I are slowly cleaning what's still left of our lovely nursery, we hear voices coming closer.

It's the neighbors! And with them is Don Roberto, the landlord, who has a green parakeet on his shoulder. It's nibbling on his ear!

"We went to Don Roberto's house," my Uncle Benjamin says. "We pleaded with him as good neighbors; we explained that a nursery was better than a garbage heap!"

"And I gave him a gift, a parakeet, to soften his heart," Doña Ivania adds.

The yard starts to fill with music once more.

Horas más tarde, mientras mi papi, mi mami y yo vamos despacito, recogiendo lo que queda de nuestro hermoso vivero, oímos voces que se acercan.

¡Son los vecinos! Con ellos viene don Roberto, el dueño. Trae en el hombro un periquito verde que le viene mordiendo la oreja.

—Fuimos a la casa de don Roberto —dice mi tío Benjamín—. Le rogamos como vecinos; le explicamos que era mejor un vivero que un basurero...

—Y yo le di un regalito, un periquito cantor, para ablandarle el corazón —dice doña Ivania.

Otra vez, el vivero se empieza a llenar de música.

"I told them you could stay here," Don Roberto says. "Just as long as you let me and my parakeet come to see the flowers. In my country, I had a bird just like this one, but it flew away . . ."

A smile blooms on his lips, like a flower.

—Les dije que ustedes pueden quedarse —dice don Roberto— siempre y cuando me dejen venir a ver las flores con mi periquito. En mi país yo tenía uno igualito a éste, pero se me fue volando.

En los labios, como una flor, al señor le nace una sonrisa.

From her apron, my *mami* takes out a little red cloth bag. "Here's a little bit of earth I brought from El Salvador," she tells me as she spreads it between the flowers and plants. "Now no one can say we don't belong here."

And my *mami* and I, we smile as we watch the snails go by, carrying their little homes on their backs.

Del bolsillo del delantal, mi mami saca una bolsita de tela roja.
—Aquí tengo tierrita de El Salvador —me dice, mientras la riega entre las flores y las plantas—. Ahora nadie puede decir que no somos de aquí.

Y mi mami y yo nos quedamos sonriendo mientras miramos cómo los caracoles se pasean con sus casitas en el hombro.

31

The Voice of the People

Who speaks for a community? Who defends it? One summer in San Francisco's Mission District, the people in the real-life community that inspired this story spoke for themselves—loudly—and defended their rights. A woman very much like *la señora Flores* in *Xochitl and the Flowers* moved to the Mission with memories of a shop back home in El Salvador and hopes for a future in this country. After years of hard work cleaning others' homes, she set up a small nursery, Nuevo Ramize Flowers, in a lot behind her home. She paid taxes; her flowers cheered the neighborhood. But someone wrote to City Hall complaining that the business did not follow zoning regulations for a residential area. Mrs. Ramirez feared she would lose her beloved shop. But neighbors and local organizations organized to support her; together they convinced the city Planning Commission that Mrs. Ramirez and her shop were assets to the community. Should you visit the corner of 23rd Street and Shotwell in San Francisco, drop in, buy some flowers, meet a neighbor, and learn first-hand just how powerful community can be.

Photo by Teresa Kennett

Photo by Christina Koci-Hernandez

Jorge Argueta

is a prize-winning poet and teacher. Born in El Salvador, he came to San Francisco in 1980. His first book for Children's Book Press, *A Movie in My Pillow / Una película en mi almohada,* received the 2002 Américas Award for Latin American Literature and the IPPY Award for Multicultural Fiction – Juvenile / Young Adults.

Carl Angel is a San

Francisco artist and illustrator whose work is exhibited in galleries and museums throughout the San Francisco Bay Area. He is the illustrator of Children's Book Press' recent *Lakas and the Manilatown Fish,* and of *Mga Kuwentong Bayan: Folk Stories from the Philippines* and *Willie Wins,* and has contributed to the anthology *Honoring Our Ancestors.*

For all the hardworking women who sell flowers on the streets, for their children, and for the flowers of my house—Luna and Teresa.   J.A.

Dedicated to the people of the Mission District and to Holly Kim for her patience and support.   C.A.

Story copyright © 2003 by Jorge Argueta
Illustrations copyright © 2003 by Carl Angel

Editors: Ina Cumpiano, Dana Goldberg
Art direction, design, and production: Aileen Friedman, Woodberry Books
Translation: Jorge Argueta

Our thanks to Laura Chastain, Rosalyn Sheff, Carmen Ramírez, Awad Faddoul, Jr., Ivania Palacios, and to the staff of Children's Book Press. The author's thanks to the International Indian Treaty Council for their support during the writing of this book.

Printed in Singapore by Tien Wah Press.
10 9 8 7 6 5 4 3 2 1
Distributed to the book trade by Publishers Group West. Quantity discounts are available through the publisher for educational and nonprofit use.

Children's Book Press is a nonprofit publisher of multicultural literature for children. As a 501(c)(3) nonprofit organization (Fed Tax ID # 94-2298885), our work is made possible in part through the following contributors: John Crew and Sheila Gadsden, The San Francisco Foundation, The San Francisco Arts Commission, and Union Bank of California. To make a contribution or receive a free catalog, visit our website —www.childrensbookpress.org— or write to Children's Book Press, 965 Mission Street, Suite. 425, San Francisco, CA, 94103.

Library of Congress Cataloging-in-Publication Data
Argueta, Jorge.
Xochitl and the flowers / story, Jorge Argueta; illustrations, Carl Angel = Xóchitl, la niña de las flores / cuento, Jorge Argueta; ilustraciones, Carl Angel.
p. cm
Summary: Xochitl and her family, newly arrived in San Francisco from El Salvador, create a beautiful plant nursery in place of the garbage heap behind their apartment, and celebrate with their friends and neighbors.
ISBN-13: 978-0-89239-224-7 (paperback)
Salvadoran Americans—Juvenile fiction. [1. Salvadorans—Fiction. 2. Gardening—Fiction. 3. Neighborliness—Fiction. 4. Immigrants—Fiction. 5. San Francisco (Calif.)—Fiction. 6. Spanish language materials—Bilingual.] I. Title: Xóchitl, la niña de las flores. II. Carl Angel, 1963- ill. III. Title.
PZ7.A6865 Xo 2003   [Fic]—dc21   2002067720

The illustrations in this book were done in acrylic paints, colored pencil, and photo collage. The text type was set in ITC Korinna with Lambada display type.

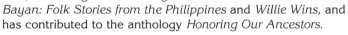